For my father, who encouraged me to travel.
For my nephew, Fergus, may you go far – *S.P.C.*

For Rosemary Sandberg – *J.R.*

JANETTA OTTER-BARRY BOOKS

Greek Myths: Stories of Sun, Stone and Sea copyright © Frances Lincoln Limited 2012
Text copyright © Sally Pomme Clayton 2012
Illustrations copyright © Jane Ray 2012
The right of Sally Pomme Clayton and Jane Ray to be identified respectively
as the author and illustrator of this work has been asserted by each of them
in accordance with the Copyright, Designs and Patents Act, 1988 (United Kingdom).]

First published in Great Britain in 2012 and in the USA in 2013 by
Frances Lincoln Children's Books, 4 Torriano Mews,
Torriano Avenue, London NW5 2RZ
www.franceslincoln.com

A catalogue record for this book is available from the British Library.

ISBN 978-1-84780-227-9

Illustrated with collage and watercolour

Set in Horley Old Style

Printed in Shenzhen, Guangdong, China by C&C Offset Printing Co., Ltd in June 2012

1 3 5 7 9 8 6 4 2

GREEK MYTHS

STORIES OF SUN, STONE AND SEA

SALLY POMME CLAYTON

ILLUSTRATED BY JANE RAY

F

FRANCES LINCOLN
CHILDREN'S BOOKS

CONTENTS

MAP OF ANCIENT GREECE

Mt Olympus •

River Tempe

Delphi
• Mt Parnassus

Athens
Olympia • Mycenae • Cape Sounio
Argos •
• Tegea
Mt Taygetos •
Serifos Island •

River Pactolus

Mt Chimaera •

CRETE • Mt Helicon

THE WORLD OF GREEK MYTHOLOGY

It was hard work being an Ancient Greek! You had to grow, make or catch everything you needed. The Ancient Greeks depended on land, rivers and sea for their survival. They believed Gods were everywhere. And it was important to remember the God, so that the Gods would take care of you.

The Ancient Greek Empire was larger than Greece is today, reaching into Turkey, Italy, North Africa and along the Black Sea. Different versions of the myths existed in different regions. Each area had their favourite gods and heroes, who were linked with their landscape. These places still exist. You can find them on our map, and even visit them yourself. Ruins of temples and palaces, rivers and mountains, can still be seen today. The world of Greek mythology is alive in the landscape.

Hidden in these real places is an invisible world. The mythical world of monsters, magic and impossible tasks. The world of Greek mythology describes another reality, where Gods are everywhere and heroes struggle to discover who they are.

I spend a lot of time in Greece. I imagine how life would have been, and try to understand what the myths might mean. The Greek landscape is dominated by burning sun, dusty stone, and blue sea. The images of sun, stone and sea appear in the myths again and again. These are my versions of those eternal stories.

THE CREATION

GIANTS AND GODS

In the beginning, Father Sky hung closely over Mother Earth. Too closely. Grass grew and flowers bloomed. But there was not enough space for trees or mountains.

When Mother Earth gave birth to twelve children, there was no space for them to grow. Her six sons and six daughters crawled. But when they tried to stand up, they couldn't. Their heads pressed against Father Sky. The children grew bigger and bigger. They were turning into giants. Titans. Their heads and shoulders pushed at the sky.

"Stop growing!" boomed Father Sky. "Stop pushing! You're pushing me out of the way."

Sky pushed back. He pushed his children down. He pushed them underground, deep into Earth's body.

Mother Earth was furious. She formed a knife from sharp stone, and called, "Children, take this knife, and cut your way out of here."

Her eldest son, Kronos, grabbed the knife. He waited for night to fall. Then, in the darkness, he reached up and flashed the blade. Kronos slashed at Sky, slicing Sky away from Earth.

Father Sky began to float upwards. He shouted, "Your children will treat you as you have treated me!"

But Father Sky floated far away. And the sky has been a long, long way from earth ever since.

❀ ❀ ❀

Kronos uncurled his crooked back, and held his head high. At last he could stand tall. "The time of the Giants has begun!" he cried.

The Titans ruled the world. Kronos became king and his youngest sister, Rhea, was queen. In the gap between sky and earth, life came into being.

Kronos and Rhea had a baby daughter, called Demeter.

When Kronos took the little girl in his arms, he heard a voice echoing in his head. It was his father, saying, "Your children will treat you as you have treated me!"

Kronos stared at the baby. He did not want to be pushed out of the way. So he lifted the girl to his giant mouth, and swallowed her whole. Rhea gave birth to four more children. Two girls – Hestia and Hera. And two boys – Hades and Poseidon. But Kronos swallowed them all!

When Rhea had a sixth child, a boy, she was terrified she would lose him too. She named the baby Zeus. She placed him on the ground, whispering, "Mother Earth, help me! Kronos is behaving like his father. He is afraid of his own children, and is devouring them. Mother Earth, save your grandson."

The ground rumbled. A crack appeared in the earth, and baby Zeus sank underground.

Rhea picked up a large stone. She wrapped the stone in a blanket and put it in a cradle. The stone looked like a new-born baby.

When Kronos saw the bundle, he said, "Not another one!"

He grabbed the stone, and swallowed it whole!

Mother Earth carried baby Zeus to an island far away, the island of Crete. She hid Zeus in a mountain cave. And the nymphs, the spirits of the mountain, brought the baby up.

The nymphs hung a golden cradle inside the cave. They rocked Zeus and sang to him. They fed him fresh goat's milk and sweet honey. They taught him spells to charm the weather – how to bring out the sun, or capture a streak of lightning. They taught him the magic of plants – how some flowers could heal, and some roots could poison.

When Zeus became a young man, he gathered some poisonous roots. Under the cover of darkness, he sailed across the sea, to Rhea. Zeus gave the root to his mother, and she pounded it into a powder. Then she secretly slipped it into Kronos's wine.

Kronos greedily drank the wine. He immediately felt sick. His stomach churned. Kronos opened his mouth, and threw up his children, one by one. They were all unharmed, because Kronos had swallowed them whole. Demeter, Hestia, Hera, Hades and Poseidon were still alive! Then, last of all, Kronos spewed up the stone!

Thunder boomed and Zeus appeared, clutching a bolt of lightning.

"Mother Earth," he shouted. "Swallow your son and save the world!"

The ground rumbled, earth opened up, and Kronos was pulled underground, down to a fiery prison, where he still remains.

Then Zeus cried, "The time of the Giants is over. Let the time of the Gods begin!"

@@ ⁀ @@

Now Gods ruled the world.

Zeus became God of the Sky. King of Heaven. Shining ruler of all.

Hades became God of the Underworld. Lord of the Dead.

Poseidon became God of the Sea, making waters wild and calm.

The three brothers, guardians of sun, stone and sea, were joined by their sisters.

Demeter became Goddess of Grain, making crops grow.

Hestia became Goddess of the Home.

Hera became Zeus's wife, Queen of Heaven.

The Gods built a palace on the snowy peaks of Mount Olympus, the highest mountain in Greece. More Gods were born.

Athena, Goddess of War and Wisdom.

Hephaestus, Blacksmith God of Fire.

Apollo, God of Music and Light.

Hermes, the Messenger God.

Aphrodite, Goddess of Love.

Pan, God of Nature.

Zeus picked up the stone and hurled it into the air. The stone landed in the centre of the earth, on Mount Parnassus.

"The belly button of the world!" said Zeus. "Build a temple round the stone, so the stone can speak."

The Temple of Delphi was built. And people visited the magic stone, asked it questions, and listened to its reply.

The twelve Olympian Gods lived on the mountain-top, in a palace of marble and gold. The mountain-top was always shrouded in mist, so that humans could not see the Gods. But sometimes the Gods parted the clouds, looked down on Earth, and interfered.

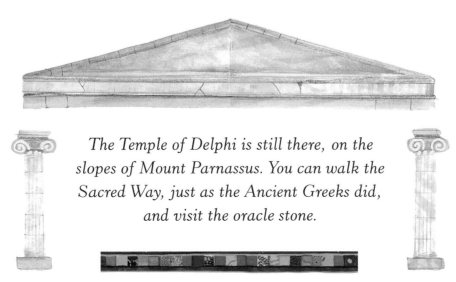

The Temple of Delphi is still there, on the slopes of Mount Parnassus. You can walk the Sacred Way, just as the Ancient Greeks did, and visit the oracle stone.

THE GIRL OF ALL GIFTS

PANDORA

After Kronos had gone, the other Titans took flight. Some giants hid in the mountains, holding up rocks and cliffs. One giant hid at the bottom of the ocean, creating the tides. Other giants lived among the stars, spinning the universe, keeping the stars in their orbits. One giant held up the sky.

Two giants, Prometheus and his brother Epimetheus, hid among the trees. Prometheus grasped a handful of red clay and squeezed it between his huge fingers. He rolled out sausage shapes and little balls. He stuck them together, forming heads and bodies, arms and legs. He wet the clay and smoothed out the joins. The figures wriggled, jiggled, and came to life. Prometheus had made people. Human beings!

The two giants loved playing with the little people. But they noticed that the people got cold. Their bodies were not covered with fur or wool, like animals, and at night the little people shivered.

So, early one morning, Prometheus stretched his arm up high. He reached beyond Mount Olympus, higher and higher, to the bright sun. He stole one of the sun's burning flames, and gave it to the little people. Now human beings had fire! They were warm. They cooked their food, and sat cosily round the fire at night, telling stories.

Zeus smelled roasting meat. He parted the clouds on top of Mount Olympus, looked down, and saw fires burning.

"The sun belongs to me!" he cried. "How dare you steal my fire. You will be punished."

Zeus ordered the Blacksmith God, Hephaestus, to forge a girl.

Hephaestus could make anything. He had even forged a set of mechanical servants to help him work. Hephaestus went to his smithy, and the Gods crowded round to watch. The mechanical servants put wood on the fire and pumped the bellows. Then Hephaestus gripped his hammer and took up his tongs. He pounded metal. He tapped and beat, his back hunched, as he hammered out a gleaming, glowing girl!

Zeus breathed on the girl, and she came to life.

"I will give her a gift," said Aphrodite, stretching out her hand. "I give her beauty!"

The girl's hair grew long, black and curly. Her eyes shone, and her mouth became rosy.

"I will clothe her," said Athena, weaving a gown of silver thread.

"I'll dress her," said Hera, pinning the robe at the girl's shoulders with brooches of gold.

Then Hestia braided the girl's hair, and placed a garland of flowers on her head.

"This girl is the perfect trap," said Zeus.

"But there's something missing," said Hermes, the trickster, his mouth twisting into a smile. "I give her the gift of curiosity."

"Her name is Pandora," said Zeus. "It means 'all gifts'. I have one last gift for her."

Zeus gave Pandora a painted pottery jar, with a lid sitting neatly on top. "Whatever you do, Pandora," said Zeus, "do not open the jar."

Hermes grinned.

And, clutching the jar, Pandora was sent down to Earth.

"Let's see what gifts this girl will give," said Zeus.

The giant Epimetheus found Pandora walking alone through

the forest. "Where have you come from?" he asked. "You're not one of our people?"

Pandora shook her head. Epimetheus took her home to his brother.

Prometheus said, "She can't stay. She might be a trap sent by the Gods."

But Epimetheus had fallen in love with Pandora's divine beauty, and would not let her go. So Pandora stayed and became his wife.

@@ @@ @@

Pandora always kept the painted jar beside her. Sometimes she ran her fingers round the lid, and wondered what was inside. She remembered Zeus's warning, and did not open the jar. But she grew more and more curious. She shook the jar, and heard something beating inside. She put her ear against the jar, and heard voices. Tiny voices, calling, "Let us out! Let us out of here!"

Curiosity burned Pandora. She had to know what was inside the jar. And, one day, she lifted the pottery lid.

She heard a whirring sound. Tiny winged creatures burst from the pot. They had stings and beaks, pointed noses and sharp tails. They were the evils of the world. The evils filled the air, buzzing round Pandora's head.

Pandora was terrified and slammed down the lid. But it was too late – the evils had escaped. Sorrow, Hatred, Cheating, Jealousy and Sickness flew off across the world.

Zeus and Hermes parted the clouds and watched.

"No giant or human is safe from Pandora's gifts," laughed Hermes.

"We've punished them all!" said Zeus.

Then a faint voice called from the jar, "Please let me out."

"Never!" cried Pandora. "I will never open that jar again."

"But I am Hope," said the voice. "Let me out, and no evil will be truly bad."

Pandora lifted the lid a crack, and peeped inside. She saw a tiny creature with golden wings and a sweet face.

"Let me out and I will help the world."

Pandora lifted the lid, and Hope fluttered into the air. Her wings brushed Pandora's eyes, and Pandora felt happy again.

ⓞ ∞ ⓞ

Hope was Pandora's most important gift. Even though humans face all kinds of difficulties, Hope always encourages us. We have Hope in times of trouble, Hope that we won't give up. We have sweet Hope that things will get better.

Pottery jars were an important part of Ancient Greek culture. Pots were used in houses and temples, markets and palaces, for storing wine, oil, water, and grain. Many of the pots were painted with stories of the Gods.

OLIVE TREE OR SALTY SEA?

ATHENA AND POSEIDON

Athena stroked her grey owl. "Find me a city," she whispered, "where I can rule."

Then she parted the clouds on top of Mount Olympus, and the owl opened its wings and swooped over Earth. The owl hunted, searching the land with its large eyes, until it came to a city by the sea. The owl hooted three times.

Athena flashed down from heaven and landed on a towering rock, high above the city. She stamped her foot on the dusty stones and an olive tree appeared, covered in green leaves and dark olives.

"I claim this city!" Athena cried.

Suddenly there was a whizzing sound, and a golden trident, with three sharp spikes, tumbled through the sky! It landed beside the olive tree. The three prongs struck a stone. Water gushed from the dry rock, and a bubbling spring surged across the ground.

Poseidon appeared. "I claim this city!" he cried.

"I was here first," shouted Athena.

"But they need me," argued Poseidon. "This place is as dry as a bone."

Zeus heard Athena and Poseidon arguing. His voice boomed across the land. "The people of this city will choose which God shall rule."

The people gathered beneath the olive tree.

"Choose me!" said Athena. "I am the Goddess of Wisdom. I will give you juicy olives to eat, tasty olive oil for cooking, and oil to light your lamps."

"Choose me!" said Poseidon. "I am the God of the Sea. I will give you water to drink, your nets will be full of fish, and the sea will be calm so that your ships will come safely to shore."

"Olive tree or salty sea?" cried Zeus. "Choose!"

The people of the city debated. The women wanted olive oil for their kitchens, and oil to light their lamps at night. The men wanted successful fishing, and safe passage for their ships. The women raised their hands, and voted for Athena and her olive tree. The men shook their fists, and voted for Poseidon and his salty sea.

The votes were counted. And there was one more woman in the city than there were men. So the women had the most votes. The women won! Athena and her olive tree claimed the city. The women named the city Athens, after the Goddess of Wisdom.

Poseidon was furious. He pointed his trident at the sky, and dark clouds appeared. It began to rain. A storm swept across the sea. Wind whipped the waves into a foam. Boats were tossed about, sails dragged away into the water. The sea crashed on to the shore and water thundered over fields and houses, flooding the city.

"How dare you vote for Athena!" roared Poseidon. "From now on, women will be forbidden to vote. Women will never vote again!"

The people of Athens scrambled up the rock. They sheltered under Athena's tree, waiting for the storm to pass. When the sun had finally dried up all the water, they decided to build a temple to Athena. High on top of the rock, they constructed columns and steps, doorways and entrance halls. Under a grand roof, they made a massive statue of Athena. It was covered with ivory and gold, and was the height of seven men!

The people of Athens were afraid of Poseidon's anger. So, beside Athena's temple they built a small temple to Poseidon. And further

along the coast, at Cape Sounio, they built Poseidon a large temple. It stood on the edge of a cliff, looking out to sea. Its tall white pillars caught the sunlight. Sailors could see Poseidon's temple shining from far away. And they used it as a beacon, a lighthouse, to bring them safe to shore.

But every citizen of Athens visited Athena's temple again and again. They took gifts to thank Athena for protecting them. And they prayed, "We salute you, Goddess, city saviour. Keep us safe."

You can still visit Poseidon's temple on the rocky headland at Cape Sounio. Or climb the towering rock in Athens, and walk round Athena's temple. You will see three deep gouges in a rock, left by Poseidon's trident. The spring is still there. But next to it is an olive tree. Athena still claims the city.

Women were not allowed to vote in Ancient Greece, and most men could not vote either! Only men who had money, or whose ancestors had lived in Athens for over two hundred years, could vote. Poseidon's curse was finally lifted thousands of years later, in 1949, when women could vote at last.

THE STONE SPEAKS

PERSEUS AND MEDUSA

"The stone has spoken," said the King of Argos. "It has predicted that my own grandson will kill me! I must get rid of the boy."

He pushed his little grandson, Perseus, and his daughter, Danaë, into a wooden chest. Then he slammed the lid shut, and cast the chest into the sea.

But the chest did not sink. It floated on the water, carried by the tide. The chest rocked on the waves, and Perseus and his mother fell asleep in the darkness. They drifted across the sea, until they were washed up on the island of Serifos.

A fisherman was pulling in his nets, and found the chest. "The Gods have brought me luck!" he cried, lifting the lid, looking for gold coins.

But inside was a woman clutching a small boy. The fisherman helped them from the chest. He gave them bread and milk. And Danaë told their story.

"We are royalty," she wept.

"Then I must take you to the king," said the fisherman.

The King of Serifos welcomed Danaë and Perseus. They were given chambers in the palace. Perseus grew up like a prince. He learned to ride, fight with a sword, read poetry and recognise the stars.

On his sixteenth birthday, he was summoned to see the king.

"I love your mother," said the King of Serifos. "I want to marry her."

Perseus looked at Danaë, and she shook her head.

"My mother does not wish it," Perseus replied.

"I have given you hospitality," said the king. "This is what I want in return."

"Ask for something else," begged Perseus. "Anything."

The king rose from his throne. "Bring me the head of Medusa - the Gorgon who turns people to stone."

Danaë gasped. "That is an impossible task! I will lose my son."

"I'm not afraid," said Perseus. He bowed to the king. "I will do it."

The king smiled and thought to himself, 'That will get rid of the boy.'

Perseus stuffed bread and cheese into a sack. He tied a sword to his belt.

His mother watched him. "There is something I must tell you, Perseus," she said. "Your father is the great God, Zeus. He visited me, disguised as a shower of gold. And you were born. The Gods will protect you. Ask for their help."

That night, Perseus visited the temple. He placed flowers before the statue of Athena, offered fruit to the statue of Hermes and a gold coin to Hades.

"I am a son of Zeus!" he cried. "Help me!"

There was a flash of light, and Perseus threw himself to the ground. A round, bronze shield appeared on the stone floor, and the voice of Athena whispered, "My shield will protect you. Use it as a mirror."

A pair of sandals with tiny golden wings appeared. And Hermes called, "My sandals will carry you wherever you want to go."

A black helmet rolled across the ground. "My helmet of invisibility," cried Hades. "No one will see you if you wear it."

Then the voice of Zeus echoed, "Find the Three Grey Sisters, they will point the way."

Perseus scrambled to his feet, and gathered up the magic objects.

At sunrise, he strapped on the winged sandals. The golden wings whirred, and Perseus rose into the air. "I will succeed, Mother!" he cried, as he soared over a cliff, above the blue sea.

◎ ～ ◎

Perseus flew over islands and rocks, searching for the Grey Sisters. He swooped over mountains and forests. Then he came to the entrance of a cave, and heard voices.

"Stoke up the fire, sister, do," said one crackly voice.

"I will stir the pot of stew," said a second.

"Pass the tooth so I can chew," said a third.

It was the Three Grey Sisters!

Perseus pulled off the sandals, and pushed the helmet on to his head. A dark cloud wrapped itself round him. He felt as if he was floating in black ink. And he slipped invisibly into the cave.

Three old hags were sitting round a fire, stirring a cauldron. They had straggling grey hair, and only one eye and one tooth between them. They shared the tooth and eye, passing them round the circle!

"It's my turn to eat," said the first, grabbing the tooth.

"I must see the meat," said the second, reaching for the eye.

"Ouch! The heat!" cried the third, dropping the eye.

Perseus saw the eye roll across the ground. He bent down and seized it. The sisters stumbled around, trying to find the eye.

Then Perseus shouted, "I've got the eye!"

"Why? Why? Why?" cried the sisters.

"So you'll tell me where Medusa lives," cried Perseus.

The Grey Sisters huddled close.

"Travel to the gate of night," said the first.

"Her snaky hair gives a fright," said the second.

"Wait until the sun is bright," said the third.

"Then all the snakes will sleep tight," said the first.

"Thank you, Grannies," said Perseus, pressing the eye into the first sister's hand.

"Be all right, all right, all right," shuddered the sisters.

And, pulling off the helmet and putting on the sandals, Perseus flew away.

☙ ∾ ☙

"West!" cried Perseus, turning towards the setting sun. "West is the direction of night."

He flew until he saw two dark gates. The gates of night. Perseus stuffed the sandals into his sack and walked between the gates. Looming out of the darkness, he saw a wolf. But the wolf was not moving. Perseus touched the wolf. It was cold and hard. It was made of stone. Perseus passed a lion pouncing. Then a man running. Perseus shivered. These were not works of art. They had once been alive, and Medusa had turned them to stone.

Suddenly, Perseus heard snakes hissing. He dived behind a rock. The Gorgon Medusa slunk past. Her head was covered with wriggling snakes. She had pointed claws, scaly wings, red eyes, sharp tusks, and a lolling black tongue! Perseus kept his eyes shut tight, so that he would not be turned to stone.

'I'll wait until the sun is hot,' thought Perseus. 'Then the snakes will sleep. But how can I cut off Medusa's head without looking at her?'

Then Perseus remembered Athena's shield!

@@ ᢁ @@

At midday the sun burned, and the snakes slept. Perseus pulled on the helmet, and lifted the shield. The shiny bronze reflected everything, just like a mirror.

Perseus stared into the shield and, guided by the shining reflection, he walked towards the Gorgon's lair.

Medusa lay in the hot sun. The snakes were still, and her eyes were closed. As Perseus crept closer, he stepped on a twig and there was a loud crack!

Medusa sat up. She looked about but could not see anyone.

"Where are you?" she hissed.

Perseus drew his sword. "Here!" he cried.

Medusa saw a flash of metal and whirled round, thrashing her claws. "It's not my fault I look like this," she spat. "I was beautiful once, with lovely hair. Athena was jealous. She changed my curls into snakes, turned me into a monster."

Perseus stared steadfastly into the shield. "Look no more!" he cried.

Gazing at the reflection, he slashed at Medusa, and her head fell to the ground.

Suddenly, something sprang from Medusa's neck. A shining white horse with silver wings burst from her body! It was Pegasus, the winged horse. The horse beat his shining wings, and flew away.

"What a beautiful creature!" cried Perseus. "Medusa was only ugly on the outside."

Then, looking into the shield, Perseus picked up Medusa's head and pushed it into the sack. The impossible task was not yet over.

Slipping on the sandals, Perseus soared into the air. He flew out to sea. Far below, he saw a girl chained to a rock. The sea foamed and a slippery sea monster rose out of the water. The monster whipped its tail, and opened its jaws to devour the girl.

Perseus swooped down, drew his sword and stabbed the monster in the heart! Then he undid the chains and carried the girl safely home.

"I am Andromeda, Princess of Ethiopia," she said. "Stay, so we can thank you."

Perseus bowed. "I will return," he said.

෨෨ ෧ ෨෨

Perseus flew to Serifos. When he arrived, he found the palace decorated for a wedding. But his mother was weeping. She was being forced to marry the king.

"STOP!" shouted Perseus, gripping the sack. "I've brought what you asked for. I have the Gorgon's head."

The King of Serifos laughed. "The boy has returned with a sack of lies!"

Perseus stood beside his mother and whispered, "Shut your eyes." He pulled Medusa's head from the sack. "If you don't believe me – look!" he cried.

He held the head high and shook it. The king, guests and servants stared at the wriggling snakes and red eyes. They were instantly turned to stone. The island of Serifos has been covered with rocks ever since.

That night, Perseus went to the temple to return the magic objects. The gifts vanished in a flash, back to the Gods who gave them. But in their place stood Athena, holding the shield.

"I want the head," she said. "I've waited a long time for it." She fixed Medusa's head to her shield. "Now Medusa's power is mine for ever."

Perseus bowed to Athena. The impossible task was over. But he was no longer sure who he had completed it for.

⚬⚬ ⚬ ⚬⚬

Perseus and Danaë sailed back to Argos. Perseus's grandfather was now an old man. He welcomed them and asked for their forgiveness. They all forgot about the stone's prediction.

Then, one day, Perseus was playing sports, throwing the heavy stone discus. He threw the discus hard, and it hit his grandfather on the head and killed him. The stone had spoken and its prediction had come true.

Perseus was filled with sorrow. "No one can escape what the Gods desire," he said. "Not Medusa, not the King of Argos, or me. May hope come from all this suffering."

Perseus returned to Ethiopia, to find Andromeda. Human love was something the Gods could never enjoy. Together they built a new kingdom, Mycenae. It was made of gold, and filled with love. A royal palace for kings to come.

*The walls of Mycenae were so massive, it is said that
the Titans helped Perseus to build them.
Golden crowns, daggers, cups, masks and rings
have been found at Mycenae. One of its most famous
Kings was Agamemnon. You can still walk through
the Lion Gate, just as King Agamemnon did.*

A TERRIBLE WISH

PAN AND MIDAS

King Midas had a beautiful kingdom. His palace was surrounded by lush forests, springs of clear water and wild mountains. His kingdom was so lovely that the satyrs came there to play. Satyrs were shy creatures – half-man, half-goat. They had human faces, pointy ears, snubby noses, furry goat legs, hooves and horses' tails.

The satyrs played hide-and-seek among the oaks and pines, and splashed in the cool streams. They gorged themselves on sweet cherries, ripe apricots, and fresh walnuts. Then they fell asleep under the shady willow trees.

Midas was proud that the satyrs liked his kingdom. "The satyrs are my friends," he announced. "They are free to go wherever they like."

༄ ༄ ༄

One day, Midas was walking through the forest when he heard a terrible howl. He found a satyr tied to a tree. The poor creature's hooves were bound together with rope, and a crown of daisies hung over its ears.

"Who played this cruel joke?" cried Midas. "It's not funny."

Midas unbound the satyr. The creature shook its ears and tail, and stumbled away.

Suddenly the trees rustled, there was a gust of wind, and another satyr appeared. He was large, with horns, a pointed beard, bright eyes and a wide smile. It was Pan, the God of Nature, leader of the satyrs.

"Thank you for your kindness, King Midas," said Pan. "My people are grateful for your protection. I want to give you something in return. You may have one wish."

Midas gasped.

But Pan nodded. "You can have anything you like."

Midas closed his eyes and thought. "One wish… only one… use it and it's gone…. I must choose something I can have over and over again."

Midas's eyes grew round. He had thought of one wish, one very big wish. "I wish," said Midas, "that everything I touch turns to gold!"

Pan scraped the ground nervously with his hooves. "Is that wise?" he asked.

"Isn't it wise to have so much gold you can give it away?" said Midas.

"Well, if you're sure," said Pan. He reached a brown finger towards Midas, and gently touched his forehead. "May all you touch turn to gold."

And Pan disappeared into the trees.

☙☙ ᖷ ☙☙

Midas turned to walk back to the palace, and the grass under his feet crunched. He looked down, and the grass had turned to glittering gold! Midas left a trail of golden footprints behind him. He passed a tree, touched it, and the leaves tinkled. The branches, twigs and trunk had turned to gold.

Midas shouted with joy. "Gold! Gold! Gold!"

He stepped through the palace door and it gleamed, golden. He touched walls, floors, tables, chairs, beds, windows, carpets, until the whole palace glittered and shone.

Then Midas felt thirsty. He reached towards a pottery jug, to pour himself a cup of water, and the water became a golden lump at the bottom of the jug. Midas felt hungry. He picked up a crust of fresh white bread, and it turned hard and gold in his hands. He reached towards a bowl of fruit, and the peaches turned to gold.

Midas stared in dismay. He looked around at all the gold, and realised he would not be able to eat anything. Not food, or wine, or water. Whatever he touched would turn to gold. He would not be able to bathe, or pat his dogs, or shake hands with a friend. He was rich, but he would go hungry. He would be surrounded by gold, but would starve to death.

Then Midas heard a voice.

"Daddy! Daddy!"

It was his daughter.

"Daddy!" called the princess. "Something amazing has happened. My bedroom has turned to gold!"

The princess skipped towards the king. And Midas backed away. "It looks so beautiful, Daddy."

"Don't touch me!" shouted Midas.

But it was too late. The princess threw herself into the king's arms. Instantly her dark hair, warm, brown skin, sparkling eyes and living heart turned to gold. His own daughter had become a golden statue. Midas let out a loud cry, and ran out of the palace, into the forest.

"Pan!" cried Midas. "Great Pan, please help me. I have been

greedy. A golden touch is a terrible wish. It is not wise at all. I beg you, take back the wish."

There was a rustle, and Pan appeared. "Climb the mountain and find the River Pactolus. There you may wash your wish away."

Midas clambered up the mountain, turning rocks and plants to gold. He came to a green river and plunged in. The water did not become gold. Midas splashed. He dipped his head under the cool ripples, and washed his greed away. When he felt he was clean, he stepped on to the river bank, and the grass remained green.

Midas walked home. Everything seemed beautiful. The flowers, and even the rocks, seemed to shine with different colours. And waiting for Midas was his daughter. Her living, beating heart was worth all the gold in the world.

The Ancient Greeks believed that Midas left fragments of gold in the River Pactolus. And in 630 BC, the world's first golden coins were made from gold deposits found in the mud of the River Pactolus!

THE FLYING HORSE

PEGASUS

Pegasus beat his silver wings and soared into the air. The shining, white horse flew over the sea, his tail streaming in the wind. Pegasus bounded over islands far below. He flew towards the mainland, swept down and landed on the slopes of Mount Helicon.

The horse struck a stone with his silver hoof, and a fountain of sparkling water gushed from the dry rock. Pegasus drank, splashed his coat and washed his wings. Then the horse whinnied. Now, anyone who drank from his spring – the Horse's Fountain – would be inspired.

Pegasus flew over villages and kingdoms. People sometimes caught a glimpse of him flying overhead. But the horse was so swift, no one could catch him.

⚅ ⚇ ⚅

One young boy, Bellerophon, gazed up at the sky every night, searching for the winged horse. He had seen a flash of silver once, and was sure it was Pegasus racing by. As Bellerophon fell asleep, he whispered, "Goddess Athena, let me ride the flying horse."

One night, Bellerophon dreamt that Athena heard his prayer. She stood before him and said, "Young warrior, you will fly. Use my bridle and the horse will obey!"

When Bellerophon awoke, a bridle made of shining gold was lying beside him. "Athena has given me her blessing!" he cried, clutching the bridle and leaping to his feet. "All I have to do is find Pegasus!"

Bellerophon said goodbye to his family. His mother wept, and his father shook his head in dismay.

"This is a foolish idea," cried his father. "No one can catch Pegasus."

Bellerophon walked through heat and dust to Mount Helicon. He waited beside the Horse's Fountain. The flying horse did not appear. Days turned to weeks, but Bellerophon did not give up.

Then, one evening, he heard a rushing sound. Wind buffeted him and two huge, silver wings circled above his head. Bellerophon dived behind a bush, and the flying horse swooped to the ground!

As the horse bent his head to drink, Bellerophon jumped from his hiding place. He threw the golden bridle over Pegasus's neck and pulled it tight. The horse beat his wings and tried to fly away. Bellerophon clung to the bridle. Pegasus bucked and kicked, and at last became still.

Bellerophon stroked the horse's glossy head and said, "You're mine now."

He climbed on to the horse's back. He shook the bridle, Pegasus beat his wings, and they soared into the sky.

"Whoo hoo!" shouted Bellerophon, as they rose over the mountain top and raced towards the sea. Like a streak of silver flashing through the sky, horse and rider had become one.

❦ ❦ ❦

The horse responded to the lightest touch, galloping and turning at the rider's command. Bellerophon and Pegasus flew east,

over islands and sea. Then, way down below, the young warrior saw a land devastated by fire. Fields and houses had been burned black. Bones lay strewn over the side of a mountain.

Bellerophon gripped the bridle and brought Pegasus down to the ground. Crowds ran to greet them, to marvel at the winged horse and offer them hospitality.

"Thank you for your welcome!" said Bellerophon. "But what has happened to your land?"

The crowd fell silent, and an old man stepped forward. "We are terrified," he said. "A monster lives on the mountain – the Chimera, with three heads. It breathes fire. It has eaten our sheep and cows. And now it is eating people. We sent our soldiers to kill it. But their swords could not cut it, and their arrows bounced from its back. All our soldiers were devoured."

"I will fly over it," said Bellerophon, "and do what I can. I will need weapons – spears and arrows, and a large lump of lead."

来 来 来

By evening, sacks of weapons had been loaded on to Pegasus's back. Bellerophon shook the bridle, and they soared into the sky, turning towards the monster's mountain.

In the distance flames flashed. The whole mountain was on fire. On the highest peak stood the Chimera, surrounded by flames. It had the body of a lion and a dragon's tail. Three heads, breathing fire, twisted from one neck. A roaring lion on one side. A giant goat with towering horns on the other. And in the centre, a writhing serpent with pointed fangs.

Bellerophon steered Pegasus above the monster. He hurled spears at it, but the spears would not pierce the Chimera. The three mouths opened wide, letting out a fire-breath, shooting flames into the sky. Horse and rider were blasted with fire.

૭૭ ૦૦ ૭૭

Bellerophon rode Pegasus higher. "There is only one way to kill this beast," said the warrior.

He pulled an arrow from the sack and jammed a lump of lead on to the tip. Then he flew Pegasus as close as he dared. As the three mouths opened, Bellerophon aimed at the hissing serpent. He loosed the arrow, and it flew straight down the serpent's throat. The fiery throat melted the lead. Molten lead ran down the monster's throat

and into its belly, scalding and burning it, from the inside out!

The Chimera fell to the ground, writhing. Then it died, consumed in its own flames. Those flames were so hot – they have never gone out. Those flames are still burning to this very day!

❦ ❦ ❦

Bellerophon was a hero! A wreath of olive leaves was placed on his head. A banquet was held in his honour. He was given bags of gold, jugs of olive oil, barrels of wine. Everywhere he went people invited him into their homes. Bellerophon had become famous.

One night, Bellerophon stroked Pegasus and said, "This town is too small, my steed. There is only one place good enough for us."

Bellerophon leapt on to the horse, seized the bridle and steered Pegasus north, to Mount Olympus. "We're going to live with the Gods!" he cried. "Only heaven is big enough for us!"

He urged Pegasus up Mount Olympus, towards the snowy peak. "Now we can look into heaven," cried Bellerophon, "and see if the Gods really exist!"

❦ ❦ ❦

On top of Mount Olympus, Zeus heard beating wings. He parted the clouds, and saw Bellerophon riding Pegasus.

"No, proud lad," laughed Zeus. "No human can see the home of the Gods. You have forgotten that pride comes before a fall."

Zeus circled his hand in the air, and a horse-fly appeared. A nasty fly with a sharp sting. The fly buzzed out of heaven, down the mountain, under Pegasus's tail, and stung his bottom! The horse reared up, tossing Bellerophon from his back.

Bellerophon plummeted towards the ground. Athena was watching, and quickly placed a pile of soft moss on the ground. Bellerophon landed on the moss and survived. But he spent the rest of his life looking for Pegasus, wandering the world, searching for his winged horse.

இ௸ ௸ ௸

Pegasus carried on flying, up and up, higher and higher. Past the snow, through the clouds, and over the golden halls of heaven.

Pegasus did not stop. He flew on, past the moon, and into space. Pegasus became a constellation of stars. A group of silver stars in the shape of a horse, that is still flying across the night sky.

The story of Bellerophon might be the source of the story of Saint George and the dragon. But for the Ancient Greeks, the story was about 'hubris', pride. And it shows what happens when a hero thinks he is more important than the Gods.
The Horse's Fountain is known as the 'Hippokrene', and is still on Mount Helicon.
You can visit Mount Chimera in Southern Turkey, and see what the monster left behind. Fire continually flickers and flashes from holes all over the mountain.

THREE GOLDEN APPLES

ATALANTA

"A baby girl!" laughed the queen, tickling the baby's soft cheeks. The Queen of Tegea wrapped her daughter in a blanket. Then she carried her through the marble corridors of the palace.

She showed the bundle to the king. "You have a little princess!"

"A girl," said the king. "But I wanted a son. A boy to rule my kingdom."

The queen opened the blanket. "See how beautiful she is. She has green eyes! And look, she already has little golden curls. Shall we call her Atalanta?"

"I have no use for a girl," said the king. He called a soldier, and pressed the baby into the soldier's arms. "Get that girl out of here. Take her to Mount Taygetos and leave her."

The queen wept. But baby Atalanta was carried away.

❀❀ ❀ ❀❀

The soldier tucked the baby into his saddle, and rode towards the mountain. Mount Taygetos was high, and its peak was covered in snow. The soldier put the bundle down on to bare rock. And his heart filled with fear. He knew the baby would be eaten by wild beasts.

It grew cold and dark. Wolves howled, and Atalanta began to cry. A huge, brown bear appeared. The bear sniffed the bundle, and opened her jaws. But she did not bite. She softly picked the bundle up in her large muzzle, and carried it to her cave.

Three little bear cubs bounded from the cave, to greet their mother. They were hungry, and mother bear and cubs tumbled to the ground. While the cubs suckled milk, the mother bear gently opened the bundle with her claws. Then she rolled the baby on to her furry tummy, and fed Atalanta bear's milk!

Atalanta drank bear's milk, and grew strong. The mother bear gave the baby herbs, honey and raw fish to eat. As Atalanta grew, the bear cubs taught her to crawl and wrestle, jump and run. Atalanta learned the language of bears, grunting, purring and growling. She wore an old bear-skin over her shoulders like a furry cloak. The bears had become her family.

@@ ~ @@

Atalanta lived with the bears for fourteen years. Then, one day, a group of hunters saw something running over the rocks.

"Is that human or bear?" asked one hunter.

The hunters watched the creature leaping over boulders.

"Bears don't run that fast," said another hunter. He pulled a chunk of bread from his sack and threw it on the ground.

Atalanta dashed forward, grabbed the bread, stuffed it into her mouth, then spat it out. She'd never tasted bread before, and she didn't like it!

"What's your name, girl?" asked the hunter.

Atalanta stared blankly. She did not understand human speech.

The hunters brought the bear-girl food and clothes, and gradually taught her to speak. Atalanta ate cooked food. She learned to shape words with her mouth. She dressed in human robes. But she would not wear the shoes the hunters brought. The shoes felt heavy on her feet. They slowed her down.

News travelled about the girl brought up by bears. Even the King of Tegea heard about her. And he wondered, 'Could this bear-girl be my Atalanta?'

Fourteen years had passed since he had banished his daughter to the mountains. His queen had died, and he was lonely. The King of Tegea ordered the hunters to bring the bear-girl to the palace.

A tall girl, with long legs, green eyes, and a tangle of golden curls stood before the king. She was calm, radiant and strong.

Tears filled the king's eyes. "You look just like your mother," he whispered. "You are my daughter. And a princess. Your name is Atalanta." He bowed his head in shame. "I cruelly sent you to the mountains to die. If you can forgive me, come home. And take the throne. It belongs to you."

Atalanta took her father's hand. "The bears taught me to love family first. I forgive you, Father. I will honour you, as I honour my mother in the forest."

来 来 来

Atalanta became the Queen of Tegea. Instead of sitting on the throne, she ran through the palace. She raced through the gardens. She sprinted through the streets. But she refused to wear shoes. She ran barefoot, and everyone cheered as she dashed past, amazed by her speed.

"Father!" cried Atalanta, catching her breath. "The kingdom loves to see me run. Let's have a running race. The prize can be me. If any man can run faster than me – I will marry him!"

Her father frowned. "Any man? But you can't marry *any* man – you're the queen."

"I won't be marrying anyone," laughed Atalanta. "No one can run faster than me!"

So the competition was announced. All the young men wanted to marry Atalanta, and they lined up to race.

"On your marks… get set… GO!" cried the king.

The men ran fast. But Atalanta was faster. She was so swift, her feet barely touched the ground. No one could keep up with her. She flashed past the other runners, and crossed the finishing line first.

The crowd cheered!

"What fun!" cried Atalanta. "Let's do it again, and I'll give you all a head-start."

"Get set… GO!" shouted the king.

The young men set off first, racing hard. When they were half-way round the track, Atalanta started to run. Her stride was long. She sprinted, caught up with them, then overtook them. Running like the wind, she finished far ahead.

The crowd went wild.

☞ ☜ ☞

The race became a regular event, and huge crowds gathered to watch Atalanta run, and win.

Among the crowds was young Melanion. He always stood at the finishing line, to see Atalanta dash past. Melanion longed to join the race. He trained every day, trying to improve his speed. He pushed himself hard, running further and faster. But he knew he could not beat Atalanta. And he did not want to lose, because he had fallen in love with her.

Melanion went to the temple. He placed flowers on the altar and prayed. "Aphrodite, Goddess of Love. I love Atalanta. Help me win."

On top of Mount Olympus, Aphrodite parted the clouds, and looked down on Earth. "I know when love is true," she murmured. "This love deserves my help."

Aphrodite flashed over sky and sea, to the Western Ocean at the edge of the world. There was a little island. On it stood an apple tree, covered with shining, golden apples. Aphrodite flew down, and touched three golden apples.

Instantly, three gleaming apples appeared on the altar, before Melanion. Aphrodite's sweet voice echoed though the temple. "Take the apples, use them well."

Melanion picked up the apples. They were hard, heavy, and made of solid gold.

At the next race, Melanion stood at the starting line, the three apples hidden in his tunic.

"GO!" shouted the king.

Melanion ran with all his power. Atalanta was swift, and soon caught up with him. She was about to overtake him, when Melanion pulled an apple from his tunic and dropped it at her feet. Melanion did not have time to see if Atalanta stopped. He ran on, as fast as he could.

But Atalanta saw something shiny roll across her path. "What beauty is this?" she cried. And she bent to pick up the golden apple.

Melanion ran ahead. Within moments Atalanta was beside him. He quickly rolled the second apple to the ground.

"Another enchanted fruit!" laughed Atalanta, and she stopped to seize the shimmering apple.

Melanion raced on. Atalanta was about to pass him, when he dropped the last apple. Then Melanion ran and ran with all his might, and crossed the finishing line first!

Just behind him was Atalanta, holding three golden apples in her skirt. "I have been beaten by three golden apples!" she laughed. "Young man, you have won the race and won my hand."

Melanion bowed, and whispered, "Blessings on you, Aphrodite."

But the crowd did not cheer. They were disappointed that Atalanta had been beaten, because now there would be no more races.

So Atalanta declared that a new stadium would be built, at Olympia. The races would continue for all time!

Atalanta and Melanion gave the three golden apples to their children, who gave them to their children, who gave them to their children, who... Those three golden apples are hidden somewhere, waiting to be found.

The very first Olympic Games were held in Olympia around 800 BC. You can still visit Olympia, and walk through the ruins of the wrestling school, or see where the chariot races took place. You can run through the arched entrance to the stadium, and even race round the running track. But if you really want to be an Ancient Greek, then make sure that you run in bare feet! In Ancient Greece, the aim of competing in the Olympics, was not just to win, it was to achieve 'arete' – excellence. And for the Ancient Greeks, excellence was something to strive for, not just in the Olympic Games, but in everyday life as well.

JOURNEY TO THE UNDERWORLD

ORPHEUS AND EURYDICE

"Orpheus! Come and eat!"

Orpheus heard his mother calling. He put down his musical instrument, a stringed lyre, and ran through the house. He passed Aunty Terpsichore practising a dance, and Aunty Euterpe playing her flute. Orpheus ran out, on to the veranda. The table had been pushed under the shade of a tree. He sat down, and helped himself to bread.

Orpheus lived in a house, high on Mount Helicon, with views over the sea. He lived with his mother, her eight sisters, and his grandmother. His mother and aunts were the nine Muses. They inspired the arts on earth, making humans dance, act, and sing. His aunties were constantly creating something. There were always interesting things lying around – baskets of costumes that needed mending, scary masks, or poems scribbled on to scruffy bits of paper.

But Orpheus loved his grandmother best. Her name was Memory, and she knew hundreds of stories. She told Orpheus tales of her childhood among the Gods, legends of nymphs and monsters, and stories about the stars.

Grandmother Memory handed Orpheus a plate of roast chicken and lemon potatoes. "Your favourite," she smiled.

Orpheus dug into crispy chicken and oozing potatoes. "I've decided!" he said. "I know what I want to be when I grow up."

His aunts fell silent.

"I want to be a *rhapsodos*. A storyteller."

"All our jobs put together!" laughed his aunts.

But his mother, Kalliope, shook her head. "That is the most difficult art-form of all, Orpheus. To be a *rhapsodos* you must play the lyre, write stories in rhyme, learn them by heart, and sing them." Kalliope turned to Memory. "It's your fault, Mama, for telling him so many stories."

Memory wiped her hands on her apron. "He loves stories because of you, Kalliope – you're the muse of stories." She looked at Orpheus. "If you want to be a *rhapsodos*, we'll help you."

@@ @@ @@

Orpheus trained. He practised every day. He learned scales and melodies, rhythms and rhymes. He learned how to stitch stories together. And Memory taught him how to remember them. When Orpheus was ready, the Muses took him to the slopes of Mount Helicon, to a glittering fountain.

"Drink from the Horse's Fountain," instructed Memory. "The well of inspiration, created by Pegasus."

Orpheus gulped the cool, fresh water.

"May your words have wings," said his grandmother.

Orpheus gave his first performance at a festival. The audience listened, spellbound, as he sang about a boy who turned into a bird. At the end, the audience cheered. Orpheus saw his mother and the other eight Muses, clapping proudly! He had become a singer of stitched verses – a *rhapsodos*.

Orpheus travelled from court to market, singing stories. He joined

the voyage of the Argonauts and played for the sailors. His music made the ship, the Argo, move swiftly over the sea. His playing charmed the Clashing Rocks, and put the dragon to sleep, so that Jason could steal the Golden Fleece.

❦ ❦ ❦

Then Orpheus met Eurydice, a nymph who loved to dance. Orpheus played for Eurydice, and his music gained new powers. Bears and lions lay down beside Orpheus, to listen to his music. Stones rolled to his feet. Birds stopped singing. Trees pulled themselves up by their roots and danced.

Orpheus bewitched the whole of nature with his music. He took Eurydice's hands and said, "You inspire my playing. You are my very own muse!"

So Orpheus married Eurydice. Flowers were strung between trees, wine glasses lifted, and Memory and her daughters blessed their love.

Orpheus travelled around telling stories, and Eurydice came with him. Sometimes she joined his performance, dancing to his music.

But one afternoon it was very hot. Eurydice walked by a river to cool down. The River Tempe wound through a gorge filled with lush green trees. Eurydice enjoyed the shade and the sound of water. She was not scared of wild beasts, because Orpheus always charmed nature. But Orpheus was not with her.

Eurydice forgot to take care. She stepped on a clump of a grass, and a snake reared up. The snake hissed, and bit her on the ankle! Eurydice cried out. Poison swept through her body, and she fell to the ground.

Eurydice was carried through the streets. Doctors tried to save her, but it was too late. Eurydice died. Orpheus covered her body with flowers. And the nine Muses sang hymns.

Orpheus sat by Eurydice's grave. "I cannot live without her," he said. "I will go down to the Underworld and get her back."

"That's impossible!" cried his mother. "No one returns from the Land of the Dead."

The Muses begged him not to go. But Orpheus picked up his lyre and set off to the Underworld.

@@ ⌒ @@

Orpheus followed a track between steep rocks, into a cave. He left daylight behind him and walked into the darkness. A path led him deeper and deeper underground. He walked down into the dark until he came to a slow-moving, green river. It was the River Styx.

An old man, dressed in rags, held out a gnarled hand. "I am the ferryman," he said. "If you want to cross, you must pay."

Orpheus had forgotten to bring money. So he began to sing.

The ferryman listened, and, dazed, led Orpheus on to his boat. The boat quivered, listening too. Then the ropes untied themselves, and the boat slid across the water.

The boat stopped beneath towering, black gates, and Orpheus stepped ashore. A monstrous dog with three heads leapt at him, snarling, snapping and biting. It was Kerberos, the guardian of the Underworld.

Orpheus had forgotten to bring cake to calm the beast. But he plucked his lyre, and Kerberos sank to the ground. Its three heads swayed. Its six eyes closed. And the gates to the Underworld swung open.

Orpheus stepped into a hall, carved out of bare rock. Hades, Lord of the Dead, was sitting on a throne made of stone.

Beside him was Persephone, Queen of the Underworld. She rose to her feet. "Welcome, brave hero! You are the only one to come to the Underworld by choice." She called for bread and wine. "Eat! Drink!" she said.

Orpheus remembered Persephone's own story. He knew that if he wanted to leave the Underworld, he must not eat the food of the dead.

"I'm not hungry," he said. "I've come to get Eurydice back."

Hades shook his head. "The dead belong to the dead," he said. "Your wife must remain here. But you have brought your lyre. Play for us, *rhapsodos*."

So Orpheus sang a myth of creation.

Hades leaned forward, listening, a smile curling on his lips. He took Persephone's hand in his, and said, "You have lifted my heart, *rhapsodos*. I know what it is to lose your loved one. Persephone returns to earth each spring, and I am lonely."

Hades rose to his feet. "You are a true *rhapsodos*, and you need your muse. Play your songs as you leave the Underworld, and Eurydice will follow. But you must not look back to see if she is there. You must trust she is behind you. Do not look back until you step out into the light, or you will lose her for ever."

Orpheus was filled with happiness. He began to play, as he walked away. He imagined Eurydice was just behind him. He played Kerberos to sleep, and the ferryboat across the Styx. He thought of Eurydice listening, as he followed the track upwards. It was steep, and such

a long way. He thought she might be tired. So he walked slowly. He played softly, listening for her footsteps. But he did not hear them. He was afraid that she had got left behind.

Then, in the distance, he saw a speck of daylight. Without a thought, Orpheus turned. "We're nearly there, my darling!"

Just behind him was Eurydice! She was pale, and limped on her wounded foot. She stretched out her arms to Orpheus. He reached towards her, but she slipped through his hands like mist.

Eurydice faded. She became a ghost. And vanished into air. Eurydice had gone for ever.

෨෨ ෬ ෨෨

Orpheus stepped out of the Underworld alone. He never returned to Mount Helicon. Instead, he wandered from place to place, telling his own story.

Orpheus felt he had failed. But his songs were more beautiful than ever. And everyone who heard them knew that Orpheus was a brave hero. Because, not only had Orpheus gone to the Underworld, he had come back!

*Orpheus became an important figure in Ancient Greece.
People acted out his story and sang his songs.
They believed that because he had been to the Underworld,
and come back, he knew the secrets of life and death.*

A SECRET SHARED

APOLLO AND MIDAS

Apollo played the lyre better than anyone, even Orpheus! When he touched the strings, they sounded like liquid gold. Apollo's music enchanted the Gods, and they were sure that Apollo was the best musician of all.

Then Athena found a bone from an eagle's wing. It was long and curved. She carved tiny holes along the bone, and an opening at one end. She put the bone to her lips and blew. The bone made a soft, breathy sound. Athena had invented the flute! She played to the Gods.

Hera and Aphrodite giggled. "Your cheeks are all puffed up!" chuckled Hera.

"Your mouth is twisted!" laughed Aphrodite.

"You look ugly playing that thing!" grinned Apollo.

The Gods burst into laughter.

Athena was furious, and she hurled the flute from the top of Mount Olympus.

❀ ～ ❀

The flute tumbled through the sky and landed in Midas's kingdom. It was found by a young satyr, Marsyas. He blew the flute and a sweet, whistling sound came out! He blew the flute and he didn't care if he looked ugly – he already was!

The satyr practised every day. He played jolly dances and slow tunes. King Midas invited Marsyas to play at the palace, and the guests listened, entranced. The music whirled about them like the wind. They were sure that Marsyas was the best musician of all.

When Apollo heard about the satyr, he was not pleased.

He flashed down to Earth to find Marsyas. "I challenge you to a musical contest!" cried Apollo.

Marsyas was scared, and shook his furry head. "But, great Apollo, you are the best musician of all."

"That is what I want to prove," said Apollo. "We need a judge."

"King Midas is fair," said Marsyas, pricking up his ears.

So Midas announced a music competition. The audience gathered in the forest. People leant against trees and rocks, waiting for the concert to begin.

Apollo appeared and the crowd fell silent. His lyre rang out, tinkling and glittering. The sound rippled across the glade, spreading like sunshine. The listeners felt warm, as if golden light had filled their hearts.

The crowd rose to their feet, cheering.

Then Marsyas played his flute and a low sound, like gentle wind, echoed through the forest. The sound seemed to lift the listeners into the air. The notes rose higher, and the listeners felt as if they were flying! Then with tumbling notes, Marsyas brought the listeners back down to earth.

The crowd were silent. They did not clap, or cheer. They did not even smile. Marsyas was sure that nobody liked his music.

Midas addressed the crowd. "I think you'll all agree who the winner is!"

Apollo grinned, and Marsyas hung his furry head.

"His music moved us so much, we could not clap or smile.

Marsyas is the best musician of all!"

Now the crowd cheered! They stamped, shouted and roared for more until Marsyas played again. After that, Marsyas became famous. He played his flute all over Greece, inspiring people to make their own flutes from bones, wood and reeds.

But Apollo took Midas aside. "If you think this ugly creature is a better musician than me," said Apollo, "there is something wrong with your ears. I'll show you what kind of ears you have!"

Apollo brushed his hand across Midas's head, and two brown, hairy ears appeared. "The ears of a donkey!" cried Apollo, vanishing in a flash of light.

Midas ran to the palace and stared into a mirror. His ears were long and shaggy, and waggled to and fro, like a donkey! He quickly wrapped a cloth around his head. He covered up the donkey's ears, and placed his crown on top.

"I will grow my hair long," muttered the king. "Then no one will know my secret."

@@ @@

Midas's hair grew and grew. It grew so long, he had to have it cut. Midas called for his barber.

The barber removed the cloth, and took up his scissors. He was about to trim the Royal curls, when he noticed something brown and furry dangling beneath the king's hair.

'What are they?' thought the barber. 'They look like...'

And before the barber could stop himself, he shouted, "The ears of a donkey!"

"Shhh!" whispered the king. "This is my terrible secret. No one knows. Not even my own daughter knows about my donkey's ears. Keep my secret, and I'll give you a bag of gold."

The barber agreed. He cut the king's hair, took the gold and got out of the palace as fast as he could!

On the way home the barber kept thinking about the donkey's ears. He sniggered! Giggled! Chuckled! And burst into laughter.

"What are you laughing about?" asked the barber's wife.

"I can't tell you," chortled the barber. "It's a secret I've been paid to keep." He gave his wife the bag of gold, then roared with laughter until tears poured down his cheeks.

@@ @@

The secret bubbled inside the barber. It made him laugh so much he couldn't eat or sleep. He laughed so much, it hurt.

"For goodness' sake!" said his wife. "You have to stop laughing. A secret is no good for one. A secret is too much for three. A secret is just right for two. You must share your secret, and you'll feel better. Tell your secret to the earth. Then no human will ever hear it."

The barber ran giggling into the forest. He dug a hole in the ground, put his lips to the hole and whispered, "The king has got donkey's ears… the king has got donkey's ears!"

Then he covered the hole with earth. He felt better. He stopped laughing. He had shared his secret and felt a huge relief. He went home and forgot all about it.

@@ @@ @@

That summer, King Midas decided to hold a great feast, with singing, dancing, and music. The whole kingdom prepared for the party.

One musician needed a new flute. He walked through the forest looking for a reed. He found a clump of reeds, growing tall and straight from a mound of earth.

"Perfect!" said the musician. He cut a reed, made holes, shaped the mouthpiece and polished the flute until it shone.

At last the day of the celebrations arrived. Carpets and clothes were spread out under the trees, and a banquet was laid on the grass. Satyrs and humans, the king and his daughter, lay in the sun, eating and listening to music.

The musician put his new flute to his lips, and blew. A strange sound came from the instrument, a thin voice, like wind whispering through reeds. "The…king…has…got…donkey's…ears…"

Everyone fell silent and listened to the flute.

"The…king…has got…donkey's ears….the king has…"

Midas was horrified. He put his hand to his head, and his crown fell off. The cloth unravelled, and his furry ears dangled down!

The crowd pointed and shouted, "THE KING HAS GOT DONKEY'S EARS!"

Midas felt ashamed. His secret was out. He leapt to his feet and ran into the forest. He tugged at his ears. "I wish they would go away," he sobbed.

Suddenly there was a gust of wind, and Pan appeared. "My friend, I cannot take away what another God has given. So be proud! You have always loved my people – and now you are one of us!"

Midas returned, and spoke to the crowd. "Donkeys are patient and kind," he said. "They work hard and carry heavy loads. Don't you think these are good qualities for a king?"

The crowd shuffled. It was their turn to feel ashamed. These were excellent qualities for a king. "Hooray for King Midas!" they shouted.

☞☟ ∾ ☞☟

Midas stopped hiding his donkey ears. He let them dangle and waggle, for everyone to see. No one knew how the secret had got out. But the reed has been whispering it ever since.

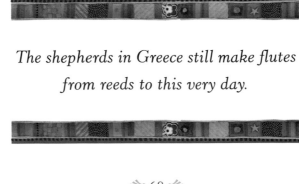

The shepherds in Greece still make flutes
from reeds to this very day.

SPIDER'S STORY

ARACHNE

Long red thread
rolled within
kick the wheel
for the tale
to begin!
(Traditional Greek way to start a story)

A golden light shone on a cradle, and three nymphs appeared. They were the Three Fates, who spin the threads of life and weave our destinies.

The first nymph held a ball of red thread. She unravelled it and said, "This baby girl will be a great artist."

The second nymph measured a short length of thread. "She will not live long," she said.

The third nymph shook her head. "That is harsh, sister. I'll change my blessing." The third nymph took up her silver scissors. As she snipped the thread, she said, "Her art will live for ever."

Then the Three Fates vanished.

❦ ❧ ❦

The baby girl was named Arachne. And like all young girls, her mother taught her to spin and sew.

Arachne was better than all her friends at stitching and embroidery.

She could spin wool so the threads were soft and light. But it was her weaving that was outstanding! She wove delicate shawls, sturdy tablecloths and carpets of dazzling colours.

News of Arachne's skill travelled all over the land. People came from far away to buy her work.

One day an old woman visited Arachne. She inspected the weaving. She ran her fingers over the cloth, to see how soft it was. She held the weaving up to the light, to see how fine the threads were.

"The stories are true, you are a great artist!" declared the old woman. "The Goddess Athena invented weaving. She must have taught you herself."

Arachne looked up from her weaving loom. "Athena did not teach me," she said. "I taught myself."

"Athena must be your inspiration," said the old lady.

Arachne stopped weaving. "What I know has nothing to do with Athena. I've learned through my own hard work."

"Be careful, young lady," said the old woman, giving Arachne a stern look. "You might upset the Goddess."

"Athena should be upset," laughed Arachne, "because I'm a better weaver than she is!"

Suddenly the old woman pulled off her cloak. There stood the Goddess Athena, wearing her blazing helmet and holding her golden shield. "We'll see who the best weaver is!" cried Athena. "Let's have a competition."

Two new weaving looms and a basket filled with coloured wool appeared.

Arachne smiled. "I know who will win!" she said.

✪ ✪ ✪

Athena and Arachne set to work. They strung up the vertical threads of wool, from one end of the loom to the other. They attached wool to pointed wooden shuttles, and pulled the horizontal threads through. They wove, under and over, neatly and swiftly. And a crowd gathered to watch.

Athena wove a picture of the Gods. Zeus was holding a glittering thunderbolt. Hades was surrounded by dark rocks. Poseidon was speckled with grey wool, like the foam of the sea. In the centre was a green olive tree. And beside it, a shining image of Athena herself.

The crowd were amazed!

Arachne chose dark wool, and wove a night sky. She wove a cold white moon, and a scattering of stars dotted with silver thread. In the centre she wove a yellow sun with golden rays that tapered into the darkness. The crowd gazed at the weaving. The moon, stars and sun seemed to move in the night sky. They were circling across the weaving. The crowd gasped. Arachne had woven a living map of heaven.

The crowd cheered. Arachne was the best weaver!

"How dare you insult me!" cried Athena. "If you love weaving so much, then weave for ever!"

Athena tapped Arachne on her head with her wooden shuttle. And Arachne began to shrink. She got smaller and smaller. Her arms and legs vanished. Her head merged with her body. Her eyes bulged, large and round. Eight spindly, hairy legs pushed out of her body.

Arachne became a spider. She scuttled up the wall, and hid in a corner.

Ever since then, Spider has been weaving silken threads and gossamer webs. But Spider really is the best weaver of all, because no web is the same, each one is unique. Spider weaves her story over and over again.

It is the story of creation. How the Gods are everywhere, hidden in sun, stone, and sea. How the world of Greek mythology is all around us.

*The word 'arachnid' is the scientific term for spider,
and it comes from the story of Arachne. When you see
a spider's web, remember that you can weave your own fate,
and make something beautiful with your life.*

Three golden apples fell from heaven,
one for the storyteller,
one for the listener,
and one for the person who tells the next story!

INDEX OF GODS AND HEROES

Andromeda – Princess of Ethiopia

Aphrodite – Goddess of Beauty and Love

Apollo – God of the Sun

Arachne – heroine of weaving

Atalanta – heroine of running

Athena – Goddess of Wisdom

Bellerophon – hero who rides Pegasus

Chimera – monster who is part lion, part serpent, part goat

Danaë – mother of Perseus, Princess of Argos

Demeter – Goddess of Grain

Epimetheus – Titan. His name means 'afterthought' in Ancient Greek

Eurydice – wife of Orpheus, who goes to the Underworld

Father Sky – father of the Titans, his ancient Greek name is Ouranos

Ferryman – his ancient Greek name is Xaron. Ferries the dead over
    the River Styx

Hades – God of the Underworld

Hestia – Goddess of the Hearth and Home

Hera – Queen of Heaven

Hephaestus – God of Fire

Hermes – Messenger God

Kerberos – beast with three heads, who guards the Underworld

King of Serifos – enemy of Perseus, who is turned to stone

Kronos – Titan, and father of the Gods

Marsyas – Satyr, who plays the flute

Medusa – snake-haired Gorgon

Melanion – hero who loves Atalanta

Memory – grandmother of the Muses, her ancient Greek name is
    Mnesmosyne

Midas – the king with donkey's ears

Mother Earth – mother of the Titans , her Ancient Greek name is Gaia

Muses – inspiration for the Arts in Ancient Greece

    Erato – Muse of Poetry

    Euterpe – Muse of Music

    Kalliope – Muse of Stories

    Klio – Muse of History

    Melpomene – Muse of Tragedy

    Polyhymnia – Muse of Song

    Terpsichore – Muse of Dance

    Thalia – Muse of Comedy

    Urania – Muse of philosophy

Orpheus – storyteller and singer, who visits the Underworld

Pan – God of Forests

Pandora – heroine who releases Hope into the world

Pegasus – winged horse, who gave his name to the constellation Pegasus

Persephone – Goddess of Spring, who lives in the Underworld during winter

Perseus – hero who killed Medusa

Poseidon – God of the Sea

Prometheus – Titan. His name means 'forethought' in Ancient Greek

Rhea – Titan, and mother of the Gods

The Grey Sisters – fortune-tellers who share a tooth and an eye.
    Their Ancient Greek name is Graiai

The Three Fates – give each human being their own destiny:

    Klotho – spins the thread of life

    Lachesis – measures the thread

    Atropos – cuts the thread

Zeus – God of Sky and Heaven. King of the Gods

@@ ~ @@

SOURCES

Ancient Sources

The Library of Greek Mythology, Apollodorus, translated by Robin Hard,
Oxford World Classics, 1997
Greek Myths compiled around 1st century AD. This translation brings them to life.

Metamorphoses, Ovid, translated by David Raeburn, Penguin, 2004
Beautiful version of Ovid's poetic myths.

Theogony, and Works and Days, Hesiod, translation ML West,
Oxford World Classics, 1988
The oldest source of Greek mythology, dating from around 8th century BC. Reading Hesiod is like having direct contact with an ancient voice. Hesiod said that he drank from the 'Horse's Fountain' and this is where he got his inspiration. Pure magic.

Modern Sources

The Age of Fable, Bullfinch, Everyman, 1855.
Romantic versions of the myths, that are part of our culture now, and known by many.

The Gods of the Greeks, Carl Kerenyi, Thames and Hudson, 1951
Comprehensive versions of the myths that draw widely on Ancient Greek sources.

Greek Mythology – an Encyclopaedia, Richard Stoneman, the Aquarian Press, 1991
A useful and detailed dictionary.

The Greek Myths 1 and 2, Robert Graves, Penguin Books, 1955
All the stories, with Graves's notes, thoughts, and references.

Tales of the Greek Heroes, Roger Lancelyn Green, Puffin, 1958
Exciting re-telling for children.

Commentaries

The Seven Myths of the Soul, Tim Addey, The Prometheus Trust, 2000
A philosophic journey into the living wisdom of Greek myth.

The Uses of Greek Mythology, Ken Dowden, Routledge, 1992
Exploring how the myths existed in Ancient Greek society.